the Three Grumpies

Alex, Ben and David—your laughter keeps my Grumpies away –T.W.

For Tom and Ette –R.C.

BLOOMSBURY
CHILDREN'S
BOOKS

First published in Great Britain in 2003 by Bloomsbury Publishing Plc
38 Soho Square, London, W1D 3HB
This paperback edition first published in 2005

Text copyright © Tamra Wight 2003
Illustrations copyright © Ross Collins 2003
The moral rights of the author and illustrator have been asserted

A CIP catalogue record of this book is available from the British Library
ISBN 0 7475 6492 2

Printed and bound in China by South China Printing Co.

1 3 5 7 9 10 8 6 4 2

All papers used by Bloomsbury Publishing are natural, recyclable products
made from wood grown in well-managed forests. The manufacturing processes conform
to the environmental regulations of the country of origin.

the Three Grumpies

by **Tamra Wight** illustrated by **Ross Collins**

BLOOMSBURY
CHILDREN'S
BOOKS

I woke up on the wrong side of the bed this morning.

Grumpy,

Grumpier

and Grumpiest were waiting for me

Grumpy jiggled the table until my milk spilled. I shouted **GET OUT!**

Grumpier squeezed toothpaste everywhere.

"Dad, I have the Grumpies today!"

"Try showing them how you feel," Dad suggested.

So I stamped my foot and pointed to the door.

The Grumpies grinned.

All three of them.

I tried to make my lunch
but Grumpy had eaten all
the snacks.
I shook my fist
at him.

I tried to pack
my homework,
but Grumpier
had
lost it.

I stuck my tongue out at him.

Grumpiest
tripped me
as I got
on the
bus.

SCHOOL BUS

Showing them how
I felt wasn't working.

So I put on my meanest face.

The Grumpies giggled.

All three of them.

At school Grumpy broke all my favourite crayons.

Then Grumpier squished my lunch flat.

In art Grumpiest spattered paint on my new shirt.

The Grumpies smiled. All three of them.

Grumpy tripped me as I got off the bus.

Grumpier kept

I looked to the right and hummed.

"Mum, the Grumpies are still here!"
"Oh dear!" said Mum. She looked a little frazzled.

I smiled a little
weary smile.

But the Grumpies didn't smile.
In fact they looked a little.
nervous.

All three of them.

So... when Grumpy made
mud in the sandbox,

When Grumpier dumped
my green beans
on the floor,

I giggled at him.

The next thing I knew, the Grumpies were waving goodbye.

All three of them.

"What a grumpy day," I said to Mum as she kissed me goodnight.

I wonder who
will get the Grumpies next?

Praise for *The Three Grumpies* …

'A great lesson to learn – done in an amusing and engaging way'
Angels and Urchins

'Every parent who has experienced their beloved child's bad moods will
warm to *The Three Grumpies*' *Glasgow Herald*

'Spirited and sharp, with witty, larky drawings, this is a highly recommended way
to dismiss bad company' Sally Williams, *Independent*

'Literally taking on a life of their own are the eponymous Three Grumpies in
Ross Collins's and Tamra Wight's book. The combination of the surreal and the
everyday is a Ross Collins specialty. Here, his angular watercolour illustrations
and ingenious layouts follow the girl's rotten treatment by the enormous
bloated creatures, and children can vicariously enjoy the Grumpies' naughtiness'
Ted Dewan, *TES*

'In Ross Collins's pictures, the Grumpies are subversive-looking blobs with
bulging eyes and protruding teeth. They are funny rather than sinister, and that is
the whole point. The central character spends all day trying to get rid of them,
but only succeeds when she begins to laugh at them. This is suitable for children
of three and over, and might just help when they have the Grumpies'
Wendy Cope, *Daily Telegraph*

'This familiar feeling is brilliantly personified in the form of three
monstrous-looking creatures called the Grumpies. Words and quirky pictures
work splendidly together in this story which everyone will recognise'
Northern Echo

www.bloomsbury.com/rosscollins